D0185149

Tips for Reading Together

Children learn best when reading is fun.

- Talk about the title and the pictures on the cover.
- Look through the pictures together and discuss what you think the story might be about.
- Read the story together, pointing to the words and inviting your child to join in.
- Give lots of praise as your child reads with you, and help them when necessary.
- Have fun finding the hidden mouse.
- Enjoy re-reading the story and encourage your child to say the repeated phrases with you.

Children enjoy reading stories again and again. This helps to build their confidence.

Have fun!

Find the mouse hidden in every picture. 

The Monster Hunt

Cynthia Rider • Alex Brychta

OXFORD
UNIVERSITY PRESS

FUN

Gran took the children on a monster hunt.

Biff saw some monster footprints.

Chip saw a monster glove,
and . . .

Kipper saw the monster!

"Come on," said Gran.
"Let's get that monster!"

The monster ran.

It ran up the hill.

It ran into the mill . . .
and hid.

"Come on," said Chip.
"Let's get that monster!"

They went into the mill.

"Ssh!" said Gran.

"I can see the monster's tail."

Gran pulled the monster's tail.
"Got you!" she said.

"AARGH!" said the monster.

Crash! went a sack.

Crash! went the monster.

The monster looked at
the children.
"Help!" he said.

"Monsters!"

Think about the story

Matching

Match the monster to its shadow.

Useful common words repeated in this story and other books at Level 2.

children come into said saw that went

Names: Biff Chip Gran Kipper

More books for you to enjoy

Level 1: Getting Ready

Level 2: Starting to Read

Level 3: Becoming a Reader

Level 4: Building Confidence

Level 5: Reading with Confidence

OXFORD
UNIVERSITY PRESS
Great Clarendon Street,
Oxford OX2 6DP

Text © Cynthia Rider 2006
Illustrations © Alex Brychta 2006

First published 2006
All rights reserved

Series Editors: Kate Ruttle, Annemarie Young

British Library Cataloguing in Publication Data available

ISBN–13: 978-019-279230-3

10 9 8 7 6 5 4 3 2

Printed in China by Imago